Susan Wickberg • Yumi Heo

G. P. Putnam's Sons

Hey Mr. Choo-choo, Where Are You Going?

G. P. PUTNAM'S SONS

A division of Penguin Young Readers Group

Published by The Penguin Group

Penguin Group (USA) Inc., 375 Hudson Street, New York, NY 10014, U.S.A.

Penguin Group (Canada), 90 Eglinton Avenue East, Suite 700, Toronto, Ontario M4P 2Y3, Canada (a division of Pearson Penguin Canada Inc.).

Penguin Books Ltd, 80 Strand, London WC2R 0RL, England.

Penguin Ireland, 25 St. Stephen's Green, Dublin 2, Ireland (a division of Penguin Books Ltd.).

Penguin Group (Australia), 250 Camberwell Road, Camberwell, Victoria 3124, Australia (a division of Pearson Australia Group Pty Ltd).

Penguin Books India Pvt Ltd, 11 Community Centre, Panchsheel Park, New Delhi - 110 017, India.

Penguin Group (NZ), 67 Apollo Drive, Rosedale, North Shore 0745, Auckland, New Zealand (a division of Pearson New Zealand Ltd.).

Penguin Books (South Africa) (Pty) Ltd, 24 Sturdee Avenue, Rosebank, Johannesburg 2196, South Africa.

Penguin Books Ltd, Registered Offices: 80 Strand, London WC2R 0RL, England.

Published simultaneously in Canada. Manufactured in China by South China Printing Co. Ltd.

Design by Katrina Damkoehler. Text set in Ad Lib. The art was done in collage and oil paint on Fabriano watercolor paper.

Library of Congress Cataloging-in-Publication Data

Wickberg, Susan. Hey Mr. Choo-choo, where are you going? / Susan Wickberg ; illustrated by Yumi Heo.   p. cm.

Summary: A train engine hauls his cars from the city to the sea, answering questions about
what he is pulling, seeing, and hearing along the way.

[1. Railroad trains—Fiction. 2. Stories in rhyme.] I. Heo, Yumi, ill. II. Title. PZ8.3.W61992Hey 2008 [E]—dc22 2006034459

ISBN 978-0-399-23993-9

3 5 7 9 10 8 6 4 2

For my son and his grampa,
the two biggest train fans
in my life.—**S. W.**

For my nephew Sung-chul.—Y. H.

Hey Mr. Choo-choo,
Red, white, and blue-choo,
Hey Mr. Choo-choo,
What are you doing?

Conductor call-call-calls.
I want to pull-pull-pull.
But I wait-wait-wait
Till my cars are full.

I'm puff-puff-puffin' *pa-fan*

In my smoke-smoke-stack. *step*

Bells are clang-clang-clangin'.

ke like

I'm on the good track!

I'm slide-slide-slidin',

Starting slow-slow-slow.

I'm chuff-chuff-chuffin',

I know where to go!

2306

9

Hey Mr. Choo-choo,
Red, white, and blue-choo,
Hey Mr. Choo-choo,
What are you pulling?

2306

I'm pull-pull-pullin'
All my coach-coach-cars
Filled with kid-kid-kids
Who want to go far.

There are log-log-logs
On my flat-flat-cars,
And fresh milk-milk-milk
In my white tank cars.

In my hop-hop-hoppers
Toys are stash-stash-stashed.
Watch my steam-steam-steam.
You-know-who comes last!

Hey Mr. Choo-choo,
Red, white, and blue-choo,
Hey Mr. Choo-choo,
Where are you going?

Through the big-big-cities
And the small-small-towns,
Got to go-go-go—
No time to slow down!

I pass cow-cow-cows
On the plains-plains-plains.
Across the lake-lake-lake
I see other trains.

Up the hill-hill-hills
Through the tree-tree-trees,
With my long-long-train
I travel with ease.

Hey Mr. Choo-choo,
Red, white, and blue-choo,
Hey Mr. Choo-choo,
What are you seeing?

There's a long-long-tunnel.
Got my light-light-light.
In the dark-dark-dark
I can see all right.

See the deep-deep-river.

The bridge is tall-tall-tall.

See the rock-rock-rocks

On the canyon wall.

Down the slow slope-slope-slope

I can see-see-see

The dark blue-blue-blue—

Where I want to be!

Hey Mr. Choo-choo,
Red, white, and blue-choo,
Hey Mr. Choo-choo,
What are you hearing?

2306

There's a ding-ding-ding
By the road-road-road.
Hear the click-clack-click
As I haul my load.

Now we're here-here-here!
The kids cheer-cheer-cheer
As I slow-slow-down
Using all my gears.

Hear the wave-wave-waves.
See the sand-sand-sand.
Feel the wind-wind-wind.
Your day will be grand!

Hey Mr. Choo-choo,
Red, white, and blue-choo,
Hey Mr. Choo-choo,
What are you saying?

I'm saying bye-bye-bye
With my bell-bell-bell.
I'm saying toot-toot-toot
As I wish you well!